Butterflies

for

Life

Balboa Press books may be ordered through booksellers or by contacting:

Balboa Press
A Division of Hay House
1663 Liberty Drive
Bloomington, IN 47403
www.balboapress.com
1 (877) 407-4847

Interior Image Credit: Rebecca Joi Jennings

ISBN: 978-1-9822-4697-6 (sc)
978-1-9822-4698-3 (e)

Library of Congress Control Number: 2020907917

Print information available on the last page.

Balboa Press rev. date: 05/19/2020

BALBOAPRESS
A DIVISION OF HAY HOUSE

Written by Liana Joi Jennings
Illustrated by Rebecca Joi Jennings

Butterflies for Life

There once was a friendly orange butterfly
who loved to float freely on the breeze.
It would flutter among all the flowers,
and fly way up high with great ease.

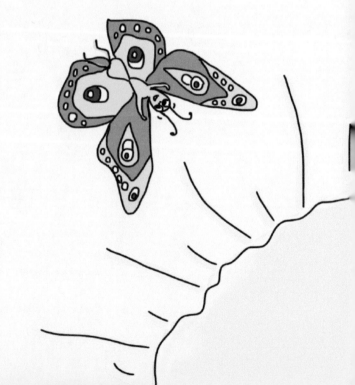

The Spirit of the wind would guide it,
up and down and all around.
Its life was full and happy,
and its feet seldom touched the ground.

One day while passing a new garden -
one it hadn't seen before,
it spotted an enchanted black spider
sitting surrounded by flowers galore.

Since it was a friendly orange butterfly who loved to make brand new friends,
it floated down a bit closer, to get a drink from the sweet flower's ends.

What it didn't know before it landed
was that the black spider had crafted a plan.
It had already spied the orange butterfly
and had wanted to get it to land.

So the black spider moved its thick, sticky web
To the most vibrant and colourful flowers.

Then once the orange butterfly got in too close,
the spider would switch on its magical powers.

"Hello" the orange butterfly said rather sweetly, "What a lovely garden you are in.

Would you mind if I sat down for just a moment?" The black spider smiled a large grin.

"That would be rather nice", the black spider said, "I would love for you to come and visit.

The flowers here are full and sweet. Please come and rest for a bit."

So the orange butterfly fluttered in closer and thought about where to land.
For it did not want to get caught and trapped in the black spider's thick, sticky band.

It carefully landed near a bright juicy flower just outside the black spider's lair.

And then started to talk with the spider, but avoided its hypnotic stare.

They were stuck! Very stuck in just one spot! Its heart began filling with dread.
Then too very soon before it could stop, it's feet were caught in the web!

The two new friends began to talk and to laugh,
for the black spider was really quite charming.
And the orange butterfly slowly began to not
listen to it's own inner voice – alarming!

For everyone knows that a black spider's web is made only for catching other bugs. And then it will eat whatever gets stuck, from butterflies to ugly, old slugs.

"Oh dear!" thought the friendly orange butterfly. "I am really now stuck in a mess!"

"Don't worry," said the scheming black spider. "You're not really in that much distress."

"For I would very much like you to stay, and become my one special friend.

You can live right here with me ALL the time, and put your high flying days to an end."

Too afraid of being eaten, and not sure what else it should do,

the orange butterfly agreed to stay put and wear spider slippers made of glue.

The black spider even would show the orange butterfly a new special way to walk.
How to glide on its slippers around the web without ever really getting stuck.

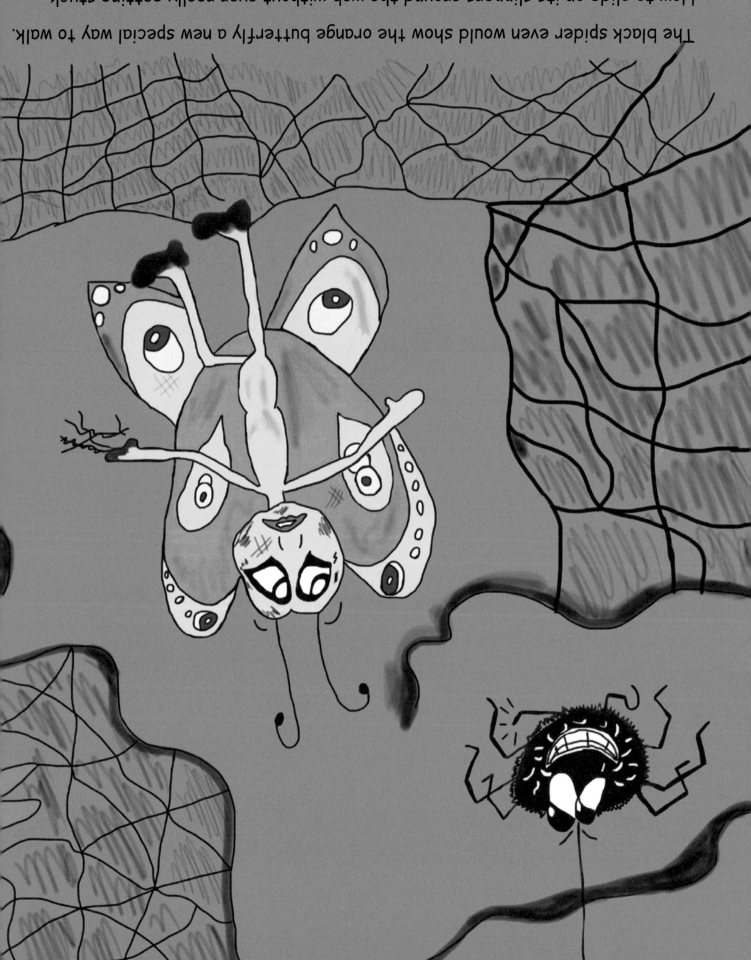

The orange butterfly began to get used to living its life like a spider, and so slowly forgot what it had been like, flying up high like a glider.

It was rather safe and unsurprising -to have everything the same all around.

So all seemed well for a little while, living there near to the ground.

Until one day, there was way up above, flying beyond the trees,

a beautiful bright yellow butterfly frolicking freely way up on the breeze.

It danced and jumped amongst all the flowers that were just beyond the garden's edge,

and wondered why it saw another butterfly living down in such a place of dredge?

For why would a butterfly want to live, so close to the ground like a spider?
When it's wings were made to carry it up, to a world that was so much brighter?
The orange butterfly now really felt stuck, and yearned to again be free!
To fly high above the trees and flowers, like it had been designed to be.

With weakened wings and a head full of webs, it struggled for quite some time.
Then slowly began to remember - And started to shake off the sticky grime.

But it also now liked this new way of life
that it had since become accustomed to.
The life of a spider - or that of a butterfly -
Oh, what was it supposed to do?

The spider looked over and said with a smirk,
"Where do you think you are going?
You belong with me now, down here by the ground.
You can't just leave me here all alone!"

Just then the bright yellow butterfly
spread its wings and flew quickly away.
And the orange butterfly knew all at once,
it must not wait another day!

So it shook its wings and stomped its feet
to loosen off all of the strings.
And before the black spider could stop it,
it jumped up and began fluttering its wings.

It took a short moment to get up high
and away from the black spider's lair.
But the orange butterfly had finally remembered
how to float and to glide on the air!

"I need to be free and to fly all around
as I was destined to be.
So I'll leave you now to be who you are,
and I will once again be me!"

"Goodbye black spider" the butterfly called,
"I know this doesn't fit with your plan.
But I can no longer sit there with you
and spend all my time on the land!"

The black spider frowned and shed a few tears,
but knew that the butterfly was right.
A spider was meant to be on the ground
and a butterfly was meant to have flight.

A spider can't fly and never should try
nor should a butterfly live on the ground.
Each one is meant to do one, not the other.
No other way should be found.

You each have your own precious life to live,
and to your own self you need to be true.
No matter what others may think or may want,
the end choice is all up to you.

Bio of Liana Joi Jennings

To define who I am, in one short page, is a challenge for me, it's true.
I'm a woman, a wife and was a stay-at-home mom, of a daughter – and sons, one & two.

My life has been totally devoted, to living and learning with them.
And every so often I would jot something down that would come to me now and then.

Old receipts, backs of cards, with crayons & pens, the ideas and the thoughts would come.
So now is the next step along for me, to share it with everyone.

I have spent my whole life learning lessons, about who I am supposed to become,
And have evolved with each lesson learned –and yet there is still more to come!

I've been a retailer, a waitress and an entrepreneur, to help keep a roof over our heads.
But my one true passion and dream come true is to be a published author instead.

I am also a singer, with a chorus of friends, who have helped me find my true voice,
Plus I love to pull out my cameras, to capture nature on film – is my choice.

I studied nutrition and natural healing once I became a mom, brand new
Then studied the art of feng shui and crystals, to keep all our energy balanced and true.

That's it pretty much in a nutshell, or in this case a verse or two,
To let you know of who I am – I'm Liana – spelled with one N, not two.

Thank you for reading this story of mine, I hope it has made you aware.
To always be true to your butterfly self, and avoid all of those spidery stares!

With love, light and a lot of laughter -Liana Joi Jennings

Liana and the Butterfly that landed on her shoulder in her enchanted garden

Bio of Rebecca Joi Jennings

This wonderful girl who was born to me so many moons ago,

Has always had a love of painting and drawing everything under the rainbow.

She's an Indigo woman who has come back one more time

And has brought life to my story that is written in rhyme.

With determined strength and quiet angel whispers

Her gentle fairy spirit helps guide all who meet her.

She's an angel intuitive and can see many colours

Around people and places, as their energy quietly whirs.

She's received her Mpsy.D Diploma

In Metaphysical Psychology from The University of Sedona.

And as a graduate of Sheridan College in Toronto

She can work backstage in theatre and other live shows.

Together we have created "Butterflies for Life"

May it bring a smile to your face and lessen your strife.

Liana and Rebecca, Toronto, ON Canada

Acknowledgements

My life has been blessed by incredible people whose love and support allow me to be everything I want to be.

My mom Stephanie, who has endured so much in her butterfly life. She's been trapped many times by charming and deceitful spiders, and each time she shakes off the webs and flies high in the sky once again. You are an inspiration and pillar of strength and unconditional love. I'm so glad you're my mom.

My brother Dan who has escaped from the trappings of many spiders as well. You are such a beautiful butterfly and I am so glad you have found your wings again. There is no limit to how high you can fly. I am proud to be your sister.

My husband Paul who has travelled beside me since the first day we met. Through good times and bad, we have flown together on the journey of this lifetime taking turns being the wind beneath each others wings. Thank you for always being beside me and for making me laugh.

My daughter Rebecca who changed my world forever. Once I met you, I knew my life would never be the same. I am so proud to be your mom and thrilled beyond words to have completed this book with your art bringing my story to life.

My son Andrew whose gentle spirit and incredible hugs lift me up all the time. Your determination to follow your own path, even when it is hard is admirable. I am so proud of the man you have become and blessed to have you as my son.

My son Ben whose fearlessness continues to show me that life is bigger than I know and angels are always with us. You are a pillar of strength and a wise old soul. I am so glad you chose me as your mom.

Louise Hay for being a true pioneering butterfly at a time when the world needed it. There are so many of your company's books on my shelves and I am so honoured to now be part of your legacy through Balboa Press and the publishing of this book. Thank you for making me a published author.

My ancestors and angels who guide me each and every day - moment by moment, whispering all the time to me with your incredible wisdom. I love it! Especially when it rhymes!

Photo Credit: Liana Joi Jennings, Liana's enchanted garden, London, ON Canada

Printed in the United States
By Bookmasters